I am eternally grateful to Euan Kerr, Nick Abadzis, Paul Gravett
and Glenn Dakin for their invaluable help and advice during the
development of Derek the Sheep. Special thanks to Lizzie Spratt,
Natalie Abadzis, Susannah and Thomas Northfield, Dad, Joyce
and family, Ashley Fitzgerald, Matt Abbiss, Dan Green, and my loyal
band of Derek fans for their boundless enthusiasm and support.

This book is dedicated to my wife Julie
G.N.

First published in Great Britain in 2008 by Bloomsbury Publishing Plc,
36 Soho Square, London, W1D 3QY

Text and illustrations copyright © Gary Northfield 2008

A CIP catalogue record of this book is available from the British Library

ISBN 978 0 7475 9424 6

Printed and bound in Malaysia

1 3 5 7 9 10 8 6 4 2

All papers used by Bloomsbury Publishing are natural, recyclable products
made from wood grown in well-managed forests. The manufacturing
processes conform to the environmental regulations of the country of origin.

Derek
the Sheep

Gary Northfield

A collection of thirteen of Derek's hilarious antics on the farm including *Gone With The Wind* and *There's No Business Like Snow Business*

BLOOMSBURY
CHILDREN'S
BOOKS

The Grass Is Always Greener

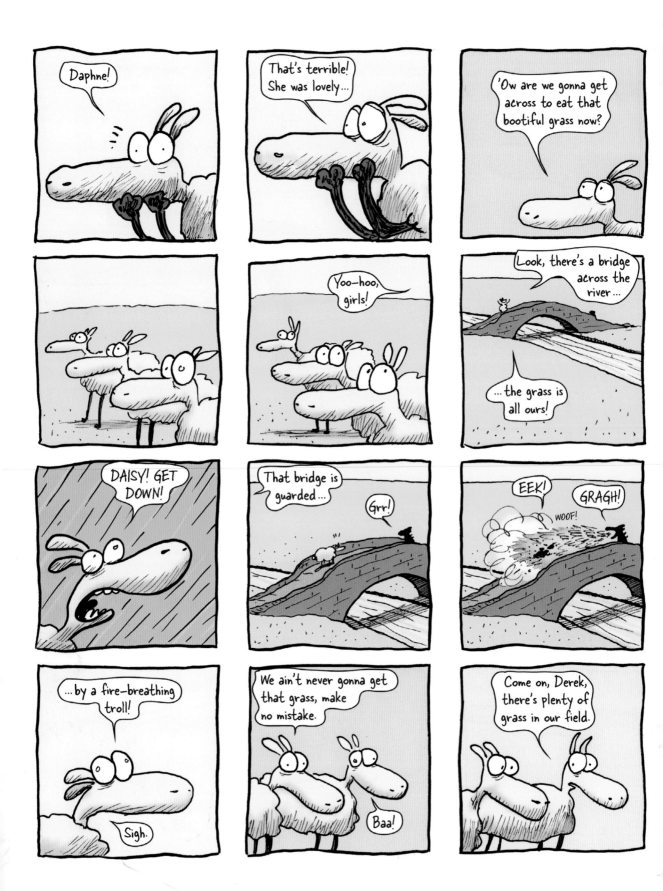

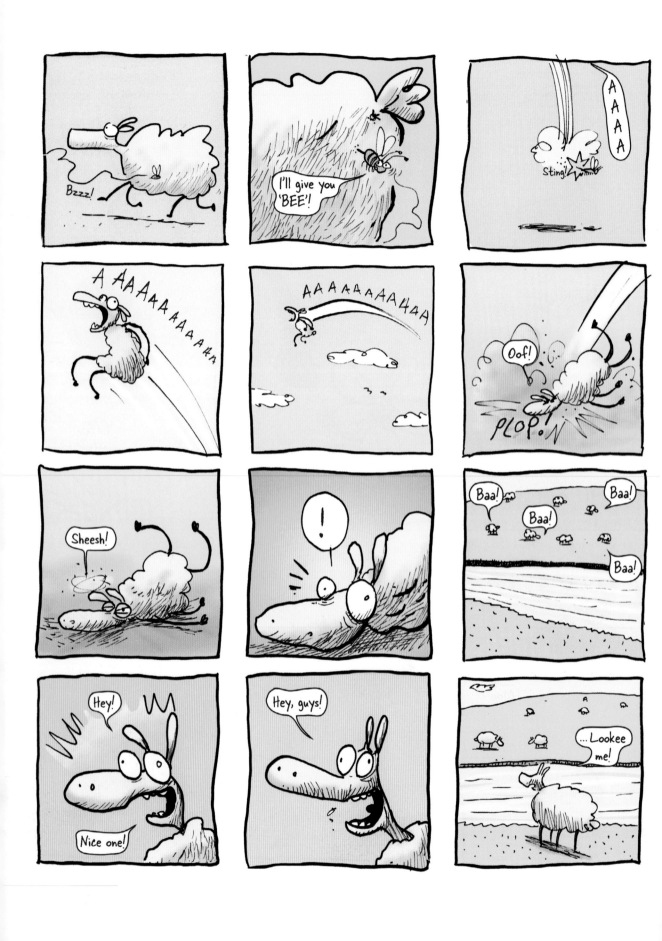

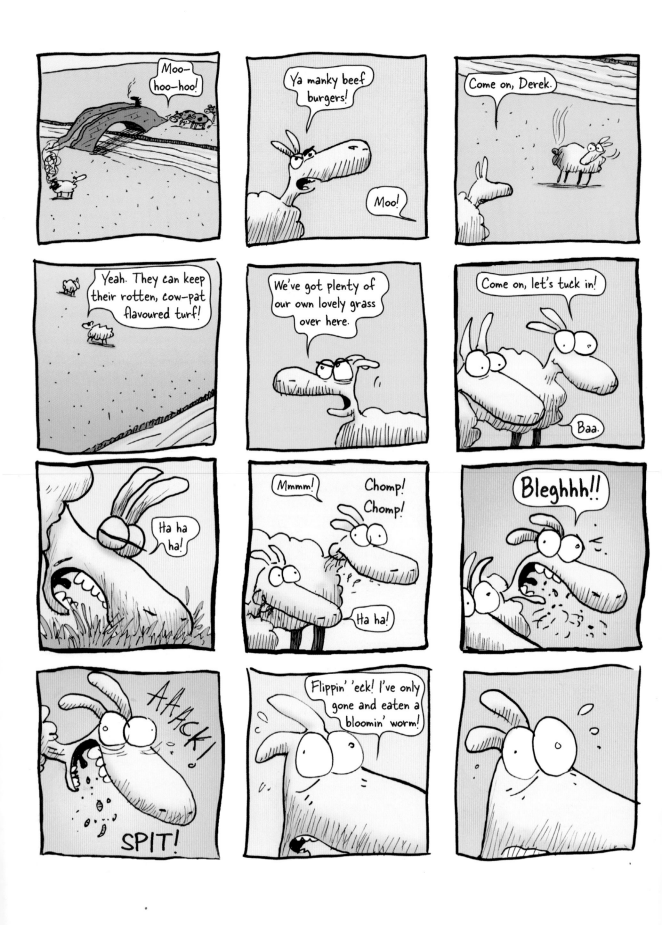

Field Of Dreams

'Ere, Lenny. Have you seen Derek today?
No, I can't say I have. Not since this morning, anyway.
That IS strange!
I wonder where he's got to?
AAAA!
AAAA!
SMASH!
I think that was him.
Do you think he's in trouble again?
BANG!
Get those sheep off my tractor!
Arf Arf Arf
Yeah! He's in trouble!
Brummm!
Pedal faster, Lizzie! Them dogs are gonna catch us!
What do you mean 'pedal faster'? This ain't no flippin' bicycle!

Gone With The Wind

There Ain't No Flies On Me!

It's An Ill Wind

He's Got The Power

One For The Pot

Let's Bee Friends

No Business Like Snow Business

Bad Hair Day

The Bells Are Ringing

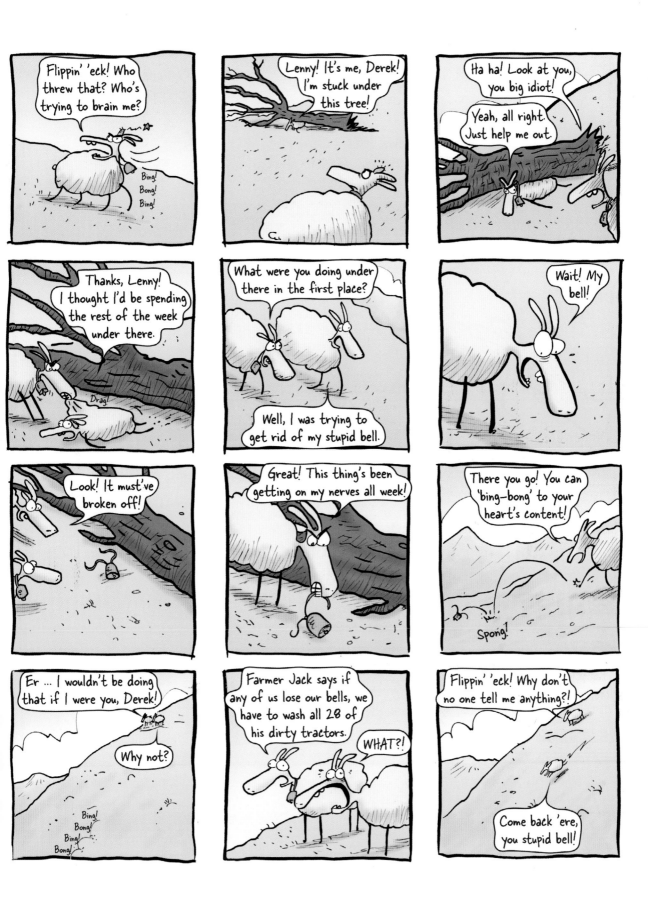

Lame Excuse

Having A Ball

Derek,
a biography

NAME – Derek Sheep esq.

AGE – 12 in dog years. Not sure how that translates into human years. Don't think there's such a thing as sheep years. (I think there are bee years though and Cecil reckons I'm 312 in bee years, but that's just stupid.)

HEIGHT – 3ft 2in.

BUILD – Athletic.

WEIGHT – Quite light. Definitely not fat.

DATE OF BIRTH – April 1st. Although there's nothing remotely funny about it, so don't bother laughing.

PLACE OF BIRTH – Back of a lorry apparently.

FAVOURITE COLOUR – Green. When I'm in my field, I love staring at trees and they're mostly green.

FAVOURITE FOOD – Grass. And hot dogs. And cheese spread sandwiches.

BEST FRIEND – Lenny, although he really gets on my nerves. In fact, everyone gets on my nerves.

PARENTS' OCCUPATION – Mum and Dad retired / on the run. Now living in villa in Costa del Sol after making lots of money selling all of Farmer Jack's top quality hay. I receive occasional postcards and it sounds like they're doing O.K.

Gary Northfield,
a biography

Gary Northfield was born in Romford, Essex in June 1969. He moved to Norfolk when he was two, where he then spent most of his childhood and the bug for writing and drawing funny stories evolved. He moved back to Essex in 1982. Gary graduated from Harrow College (University of Westminster) with a degree in Illustration in 1992. After graduation, he worked in his dad's kitchen furniture factory and an art shop for a few years, during which time he discovered the hidden world of small press (home-made) comics. Finally Gary took the plunge with his own comics in 1999, sporadically creating various titles such as *Great!*, *Little Box of Comics* and *Stupidmonsters*. He acquired the position of 'in-house illustrator' at Eaglemoss Publications in 2002, working on magazines such as *Horrible Histories*, *Horrible Science* and *The Magical World of Roald Dahl*. Gary has been writing and drawing *Derek the Sheep* for DC Thomson's *The Beano* since late 2003.